One Fingerprint at a Time

J. W. Shane

Out of Body

At first she thought the earth was shaking
>   but it was her own legs that simply
>   couldn't keep still

A tongue with an unknown hunger
>   voraciously fought to taste every
>   sensitive skin cell
>   that was normally kept hidden between her
>   delicate folds of flesh

Fingers from both of his hands found their way
>   into sanctuaries that would rarely see
>   the light of day

He brought the heat of the sun into both with the
>   aid of the fluid that flowed
>   while he savored her

The culmination of his efforts brought an intensity
>   to her senses that hinted of the existence
>   of an undiscovered form of fire
>   and the thought that she was going to be
>   turned inside out like a bud
>   brought to bloom on a
>   strangely warm winter day

Exhales rushed past parted lips

Only to be interrupted by the sensation of
        fingerprints pushing over the
        edge of her teeth
        forcing her tongue to taste the
        fruit of his efforts
        as it was known that he was never one
        not to share

Her eyes closed tightly with the fear that if she
        were to open them they would be staring
        into themselves

A roused soul separated from her skin

All of her senses were drowning and
        she couldn't help but feel like she was floating
        above everything
        even herself
        in that very moment

Crazy

She didn't flinch or
    try to stop him
Her mind had been preparing for
    that first touch
    for so long

And she wanted so much more than his hand
    on her knee

But the patience of this man

The way he made her wait

Was driving her fucking crazy

Bare

Morning slowly crept into the room
        and with it
        the heat of summer sunshine

She lay bare chested

Letting the sun and its warmth crawl
        across the skin covering her breasts
Her body absorbing the sun like a flower
        opening its petals to the first light of day
The mind behind her eyes read silently from the
        book in her hands

Although trying to put images to the words
        became a struggle
        as the memories from the night before
        refused to release their grasp
        without a fight

The warmth of the sun was glorious
        but it couldn't quite compare to the
        heat of the rain
        he brought upon her chest
        only moments before she fell asleep

Certain Dreams

There were certain dreams
      he could only have
        when sleeping next to her

Approval

Taking my hand in hers she offered
      the places that were kept hidden
      and safe
And when my fingers pushed past the
      soft
      welcoming gates of her heaven
A warmth overcame them

Much like placing my hand in a beam of sunlight

All with the approval from the god in her eyes

A Flood

The ripples in the flesh of his forearms
      cascaded like lightning from a cloud

She lifted and raised the world closer

Impatiently waiting for the lightning to strike
      her ass
      as the storm had already started
      a flood

Lather

She watched his eyes close as
    the sponge in her hand spread soapy water
    all over his skin
Making sure to get all of him clean
    her fingers left no part of him untouched
A long drawn out sigh slowly
    crawled from his lungs
    as a handful of lather that was so soft
    made certain he was anything but

Alarm

She warned him to stop talking about it
    before she would need to have him

Of course he thought she was joking

But she pulled him around the corner and
    dropped to her knees

Anything he said from here was meaningless

He felt the air for a split second before
    the heat of her mouth surrounded him
For some reason he felt like panicking
    at the movement and pressure
    of her tongue
He could feel her dragging the
    rush of release
    closer and closer

And the fact that he wasn't even
    completely hard yet

That felt like a strange cause for alarm

Cufflinks

The cufflinks were so sexy in her eyes
      and how she adored
      watching fingers work to remove them
But nothing nearly like when he was
      taking off that belt

Core

Her lips never actually parted other than
    to softly speak
She kissed his naked core while her hand
    did all the work
Slowing only when his body shook in her grasp and
    she could feel
        she could smell what his body produced
        when she demanded it of him

Turning Back

Toes were dipped in the water
      of trying something new
After the sensation of the fluid flowing
      against her fair feet
      and feeling how wet it made her
      she knew

There was no turning back

Those Eyes

Those eyes burned of
    damp sheets
    and
    sleepless nights

I just couldn't look away

More

There wasn't a way to describe
      the taste of her tongue
I just knew I wanted more

Why

She knew exactly what she wanted
    and teased him throughout the day

Poking

Prodding

Taunting him to the point of playful agitation

Standing within arms reach
    she was caught and
    brought over his knee
Showing no resistance as her panties were
    impatiently tugged down

The air felt on her secret skin was delightful

She smiled
Waiting for one breath
    then another
    and another before becoming impatient
Becoming more frustrated with every exhale

But when it happened

That first strike of his hand against her bottom
    burned with more than the strength
    he held her down with

Giggling at the first few

Whimpering with those that followed and
    crying out before what she thought
    was the last

Her eyes welled when he started again
    and her heart pounded heavily
Almost in panic because she didn't know
    when he was going to stop
        or why it turned her on so much as he
        changed the color of her cheeks

Chime

Red as blood was the
        fluid poured into the glass

Wine sips

Candlelit lips

A tongue tasting around inside a mouth
        that mine wished it was in
She gave me that secret smile as I poured
        another glass

We chimed them together

Each mind burning with what it couldn't keep
        thinking about doing to the other

A New Tide

Her skin felt the wet grains of sand
        make places for knees that were pushed
        into the beach

Swim bottoms pulled to the side
        as she slowly slid down his skin
        to settle on a
        cool
        damp lap

Their tongues shared the taste of seawater
        as her body repeatedly
        climbed and lowered
        onto his
She smiled as his fingernails dug themselves
        into her backside
Her jaw dropping as she worked to defy his grip

He cried out but she wouldn't stop

The waves were crawling away from the shore
        but it felt like a new tide was being
        pushed out from
        where she forced her body against his

Drain

Sweeter is the flavor
       that fills my mouth
       when her legs can't stop shaking

When her body won't stop quaking

When she laughs and playfully tries to
      push me away

Only for these fingers and this tongue
      to dig deeper
Savoring every drop
      I can drain from the flesh of this fruit

Tingle

Fingertips traveled lightly across her
      neck and
      face
Laying away from him
      looking up
      as his eyes
      gazed down

Leaning forward he kissed her upside down lips

Mouths opened and her arm reached around
      his head
      as tongues began to touch
Holding him in place while she pulled up
      her sundress
Using free fingers to take care of
      the tingling between trembling legs

Cricket Chirps

It was almost too much for my soul to take

The motion of her hand over
        the oil on my skin
         nearly brought a tear to my eye

She moved so quickly

But her eyes were fixed on mine

A gaze so still like the darkness that
        hung between cricket chirps and
        crescent moons
She never looked away but calmed her motions
        as I whimpered and she forced everything
        out of me

My dewdrops collecting on the
        fields of her fingers

Smiling and blinking with the knowledge that
        her purpose as the night had been fulfilled

Dexterity

She was caught in the middle
      between the softest flower petals
      and
      the cold weight when wearing metal

His imagination somehow having the dexterity
      to use both
      to subdue her body and mind

Like a painter making use of multiple tools
      to create a beautiful work of art

That Color

No

Not this time

I love that color on you

To the side
       please

Thank you

Fear

Pushing with a needy tongue
      my heart skipped a beat
She tasted like an entirely new kind of fear

She tasted like I was afraid that
      I wouldn't want to stop

As Far

Her lips pressed against him

Mouth filled to the throat
      as curious fingers crawled
Leading her hand under those spread legs
      finding his ass with her middle fingertip

She pushed
      repeatedly entering and exiting him as
      his hardness did the same while
      she sucked him

She swore his spasms were different when he
      spilled across her tongue
      with her finger as far in as she could push it

Buttons

The buttons down her spine
      were undone by my fingers
    one at a time

I laid claim to everything uncovered

Everything I happened to find
      hiding underneath that fabric

Sin

When I saw the red and black
      laying over her paper white skin
My mind could only think of one thing

Sin

Risk

Curious fingers crawled
      from her lap to his
She just wanted to touch it
      whether hard or soft

Even if there was a risk of getting caught

Blur

There was no need for her to ask
No need to guide me
I listened to those eyes as they
    led me to lay back
Everything was a blur as my pants were removed
    before her gaze returned to meet mine
The last thing I saw was her hand
    approaching before
    it was placed over my eyes
    turning the whole world black

But I felt her

That tender touch I knew so well in the daylight
    changed when I couldn't see her
She used her touch to simultaneously
    calm and excite me before I came undone
That voice of hers whispering
    "Shhh. . .everything's okay."
    as she felt my offering warm the
    skin of her hand
Using it to surround me as her
    movements slowed
    and I could no longer stand
Her lips smiling as I became putty in her hand

Lap

She loved laying her head on his naked lap
Closing her eyes and taking in
    the scent of her man
Whispering filthy things and trying not to smile
    when the details she spoke of
    made him growl
    and
    tense against her cheek

Anymore

The breathing seemed all wrong
    but
    she couldn't ask him to stop
Her mind and body being stirred by his will
Saturated to the point
    that she couldn't tell the difference
    between
    his tongue or his fingers anymore

Shadow

There was safety in the night
Looking at what her eyes could see
    without the fear
        of others discovering her insatiable thirst

Danger lurked in the daylight

If care wasn't taken he would see the
    thoughts behind her eyes
    and find that even her shadow was
    darker than his

The Comforter

He left the shower
Stepping through the doorway to find her
    waiting with a smile
Taking his hand she led him to their
    neatly made bed
    and took the towel from around his
    freshly cleaned skin and
    dropped it to the floor

Her voice wavering just enough for him to notice
    as she spoke of what was on her mind

Unsure but eager to please he crawled up
    onto the bed
    resting on elbows and knees
She stooped and kissed the skin that hadn't
    quite dried while
    working up the courage to go further
Moments passed and the tips of her thumbs
    nearly met before spreading him apart and
    diving in with a nervous tongue
There was hair of course
    but she was unbothered
    and let the sound of the growls from
    deep in his throat fuel her as she explored
He shifted his knees apart for her

She let out a muffled giggle of relief as her hand
	reached under and
	found him to be completely solid

A forefinger and thumb wrapped around and
	repeatedly worked the length of his cock
	while she lapped
	circled and
	pushed with the tip of her tongue

Minutes passed like seconds

There was no burst
There was no rush or sudden exclamation
Only a long drawn out groan

She simply felt his skin soften within her grasp
Stopping to look her eyes caught sight of a
	puddle on the comforter
Lips forming into a smile his eyes couldn't see
	as he shuddered while she continued to
	wring every last drop from him

The Light

I sat back as she lowered onto me
      with the softness of a feather
      falling to the ground
She moved on me like ocean waves that I
      knew I could drown in
When she made me
      her skin became so warm to the touch
My life flashed before my eyes as I saw my hands
      move in the direction of her breasts
And when I looked up to find closed eyes that
      slowly opened to see mine
        it felt like I was floating toward the light

Ache

The urge was so much more than the word
    "ache" could describe

They said their goodbyes

He stepped out through the door
    and her hand
    immediately dropped
    between legs that could finally relax
Checking to see if she'd soaked through
    but mostly
    because her body was
    begging to be touched

Soft

It wasn't a surprise
      no matter how much he intended it to be
Even beneath the blindfold his hands tied
      behind that pretty little head
      she knew those were her lips
None others this soft had
      ever kissed hers like they knew her so well
Her nerves on fire as all the hands present
      tried their hardest to keep her body
      guessing
She never knew what or where she was
      going to feel next

Favorite

I love the way she looks up at me
      before she swallows
      wipes her lips and
      slowly stands to close the distance
between our smiles

Ready to feel my hands on her face

Bringing her close to pry her mouth open
      with mine
      and give her the taste of her favorite kisses

Behind the Scenes

She watched the video that played
    on the screen
Lifting her ass and letting
       his hands work
          behind the scenes

Anything But

I knew that the silence she displayed was
    anything but
It was hard not to rush through dinner
    knowing what was to come afterward
We've been through this so many times before
When she showed me that smile while letting
    fingertips trace the rim of the glass
        I knew her mind was working
And I knew I'd love what she was thinking about
    doing to me

Hospitality

The weight of her was like a
    warm blanket
She held their guest while her body was pressed
    against her own

He fucked her without speaking
    as was their agreement

Using free hands she explored the body at
    her disposal
Kisses were enjoyed while her mind was tickled
    with knowing exactly what she was feeling
Sinking her teeth into the skin of her shoulder
    while reaching back and spreading her ass
    just to see the delight in his eyes

She then moved her hand underneath to where
    she could feel their bodies collide
Slowly and firmly massaging the soft flesh he was
    sliding in and out of
Eventually wrapping a thumb and forefinger
    around him
        to feel his tissue pulse as it happened

He slowed and silently withdrew

She reached into her as far as her
    hand would allow

Wrapping fingers in liquid over and over again to
    bring them up and feed their guest

She loved hosting and being hospitable to the
    special visitors
        she invited into their home

From Both

The white morning sunshine
    surrounded him with light
He stood silently
    looking around the hotel room oblivious
    to the fact that she was awake
The cup of coffee she could smell was
    cradled by his hand while
    the freshly showered cock that
    hung between his legs
    was hidden by
    the towel around his waist

She wanted a drink from both

The Way

They held eye contact
      the way others held hands
      the way others kissed
      the way others fucked

Laundry

Sometimes when he wasn't around
      she would dig through his laundry
Bringing things he'd worn up to her nose
Trying to take in a trace of his scent
      when she inhaled
Making it feel like he wasn't so far away

Fooled

It wasn't always there
But when she looked my way
When that smile lit her face
      it brought colors into the world
Hues so bright it fooled
      butterflies and honeybees
      into thinking she was a flower

Glow

An impatient moon rose so early
She didn't want to wait for the night
      to watch over us
Because after witnessing the love that we made
She loved capturing the light emanating from
      our exhausted faces
         and reflecting it as a brighter glow
         to be seen by the rest of the world

Dull

No light is the same after he'd touched her
    or her eyes had stared into the sun

Rest In Peace

Exhausted

Her drained body fell to his chest
There was a calm as she breathed while enjoying
     his final involuntary spasms and releases
     as they
     spilled within her relaxed flesh
His caress traveled over every square inch
     of her skin
     while he warmly rested
     between the legs that surrounded him

If only this embrace could last forever

If he could stay inside to keep her full

If he would be her tomb

She knew then that she could truly
     rest in peace

Starting

Arms wrapped around as he brought
      their nakedness together
Her body felt his blood filled enamoration
      push against alert skin before he
      held her near
His fingers interlocking behind
      to keep her so close

She sensed every time he tensed and
      pressed against her

That was it

Her body followed its mind and she began to
      erupt

She was starting without him

Sensation

The years may pass but never will I not cherish
the sensation of your skin on my lips

Warmth

A feeling of warmth settled over him
      as his eyes opened from dreams
      where they loved so violently

Only to find her sleeping naked next to him

Diamond

He readily responded to her words
        to her touch

She spoke of every desire that came to mind
        just to watch his body
        twitch
        tense and finally
        stand at attention to her words
She moved in close to where this desperate flesh
        could feel her breath when she spoke

That was when it appeared

The single diamond that crowned him
        sparkled in the candlelight

No more words

It was time for what was speaking to him
        to touch the jewel he was offering
The tip of her tongue lightly pushed
        through its shimmer
Moving slightly to dig in and taste
        where it came from
        inside of him

All to the begging
      the pleading
      the sights of his movements
      and the sounds that surrounded her
      screaming that he wanted so much more

Looking

Red lips were a beacon to him through
        the late evening fog
An unexpected kiss
Arms thrown around his neck in a
        reflex-like response
She didn't think that anyone could see through
        the haze her restless mind cast around her

But he could

Because he was the only one who was
        truly looking for her

Cheek

Hands joined together and they
    danced a waltz
    as each mind repeatedly
    counted to three
Turning in strange circles on the floor until
    there was no more crowd
There was only each one and the lover
    pressed against their cheek

Keys

They lay in warm sheets after
        exhausting bodies that were
        caught up in the rapture
        of that first touch
Smiling and exchanging simple kisses before
        afterglow coaxed him to sleep

It always came to this
        regardless of the guest in her bed

She would always let them sleep and
        for reasons unknown
        allow
        the anxiety of vulnerability
        overcome her mind
So much so that
        she swallowed keys over and over again
Feeling it was necessary in order to
        keep her secrets safe

Doorknob

Silence followed the goodbyes they exchanged
        until the door closed between them
Fingertips that had been exploring one another
        tried so hard to touch through the glass

He looked at her eyes

They blinked and seemed to breathe
        along with the
        rise and fall of the chest visible
        between the displaced straps of her dress

The silence was broken but eye contact wasn't

When the doorknob cried out as it was turned
Air brushed through her hair as
        the barrier was moved
Lungs taking a single breath before she leaped
        into his arms
        burying her face in his shoulder

He couldn't go

He just had to stay

Happy

Wings broken and torn by the wind
A butterfly that could no longer flutter to where
    she would find food

He found her

Picking her up and taking her with him
Loving her for who she was
Giving her all the nectar she could
    ever swallow
Her heart happy knowing she didn't need to
    fly from flower to flower to feed anymore

Sunshine

My thumb made small circles
        and sometimes drew painfully slow
        crosses over her
Two fingers
        pushed and
        twisted repeatedly
Her body condoned the thunder rumbling
        through her throat
        by quaking and covering my hand with
        the shimmer of liquid sunshine

Pleats

There are worlds to explore
      between the open covers of books
      and
      under the pleats of short skirts

Reflection

I watched the shimmer of her tongue as she
      playfully licked her lips

A reflection of light I could feel between my legs

The familiar
      sin-driven
      sensation
      that shook through eager nerves as my flesh
      crawled out from the skin that kept me hidden

I was about to stand up and
      literally
      beg her for that mouth

Comfort

His hands effortlessly held her still
Such strength could have easily
        summoned fear

But the way he wielded that power

The way that force was used could somehow
        bring about
        bougainvillea without thorns
        and force
        roses to bloom from oleander

Those hands
        however strong
        could only cover her in comfort

Rest

Lips accompanied by the hair from his face
    took the form of
      kisses on closed eyes

She lay down while the sun was still bright

Easing her afflicted body
    pounding head and
    tired soul

All in the hope that when eyes woke
    on the other side of sunshine
    a better day would be

For now he just wanted her to rest

Flutter

He didn't tell her to stop or
      wipe away every tear
His voice only spoke to say that her poor mind
        could to let it all go
        let it all out

And when the final tear fell his hands
        helped her down

Laying on a pillow feeling so much
        lighter than before
His lips kissed hers
        and his hands touched in their secret way
Making the wings on her heart flutter
        enough to worry that she might float away

Pray

My eyes closed and I
    folded my hands to pray
Her hands touched and
    opened mine before I could
Bringing them to frame her beautiful face
    shaking her head slightly

"No, no. Just tell ME what's on your mind"

Pressure

How can we feel so dull
All while sitting among the glitter and sparkle
    of diamonds created
        from the pressure we place upon ourselves

February

She warmed my soul like the surprise of
      February sunshine
The ice I held would
      weaken
      drip and
      flow
      at the mere memory of her touch
I gathered her rays any way that I could
      because every sabbatical must end
      and winter winds are sure to resume
      before flowers are given permission to bloom

No Reason

Her eyes were lost in a blank gaze that
    didn't seem to focus on anything
I held her face
    asking if everything was okay
To which she simply nodded and
    struggled to force a grin onto her
    stunned expression
She had never been loved so completely
    and her mind was simply trying to
    convince itself
        that there was no reason to panic

Honeybees

I loved so much
    so deeply
With such a portion of my heart that
    when blood found it's way from my wounds
    I would watch for the arrival of
    honeybees and hummingbirds

Chrysalis

Her eyes opened to look into his
        but they were still closed
Watching his flushed face struggling to
        catch his breath changed her
She pulled him close to rest his weight on her skin
        wrapping arms around his neck
She was ready to leave the past behind her

A caterpillar that had traveled through its chrysalis

She was intent on being a butterfly
Living among his springtime flowers
        and
        resting in the petals of blooms that
        cradled her wings in color

Heal

Her eyes lit as choices were made and
        placed onto the bed

She took his hands

Lifting them to softly kiss one of his palms
        and spoke
        "Hurt me with these. . ."
        before letting go
        touching his lips and saying
        ". . .heal me with these."

Thorns

The softness of petals grew in ferocity to
        the pinpoints of barbs
He loved with the entire rose
The blooms that stared at the sky
        and
           the thorns on stems that held them so high

The Choice

The choice was made every time she loved him
Should he be given the softness
    of an angel
      or the frenzy of madness

Reaction

She didn't always look when passing by mirrors
The only reflection her eyes enjoyed was the
      reaction of his when they saw her naked

Sweater

Slowly and easily she lowered onto the flesh
        that was standing for her

He was so comfortable

Like a cherished sweater that
        for years had been held together by
        re-sewn buttons
        patches and
        safety pins

Calming and familiar

Absolutely deserving of being against
        the skin of her chest
Keeping her warm on
        cold winter days

Page

The look she gave as she turned from one
    crinkled page to another
Reading the words in red while my fingers
    found their way into a body
    that readily greeted them
The gospel to which she clung was our
    invitation to sin

Demanding

Her hands were so demanding
One around my throat
    the other holding me so tightly
    it was almost painful
Her lips alternating between
    kissing my neck
    and
        telling my ears that she's not going to stop
        until she gets what she wants from me

Gust

A strange gust of wind manifested on a day
        that wasn't quite so blustery
Her skirt lifted in the breeze like the god
        that created her
            just wanted to see what was underneath

I couldn't blame him

Keep Talking

Shoes were removed
Legs extended under the table until her feet
     could reach him and
     slowly massage
     between his thighs
He tried to keep talking
     tried his damndest
It was so difficult to keep up the facade
     of purely meaning only business
It was unbelievably hard to keep the breaths he took
     from seeming shaken
Almost as hard as she could feel him getting
     under her little toes

Overdressed

If her skin was covered by
        even a stitch of fabric
                I would consider her severely overdressed

The Red

She handed me the last of the clothing
    that kept the rooms air from her skin
All red
    panties
    bra
    stockings

But the red she couldn't remove

The hue of her skin in places
    I loved to love so hard
That was the red I really looked forward
    to seeing her in

Kiss

I was asked to undress right there in the
        dull light from cloudy skies
She smiled slightly before leaning forward and
        placing my softness between parted lips
The special kiss of lustful lovers lured me there
But before I arrived she
    withdrew
      sat up straight and
      looked me in the eyes
Asking me to finish myself in front of her
All as droplets of rain
        tapped upon the glass of the window
        at her side

Intoxication

I drank from her mouth like she was a
    glass of wine
My entire body tingling with a luscious
    newfound
        sense of intoxication

No Intention

Tied by the wrists and unable to move
      they approached the bed with smiles that
      made me tremble

Already halfway hard the blonde
      took me in her hand
Massaging me as the brunette set a knee at each
      of my ears
She inched forward until my mouth
      became one with her while her counterpart
      slowly settled onto me an inch at a time

Heaven swaddled my senses with warmth

All I could taste
      and all I could feel was woman
      until I felt too much and
      couldn't control myself

But they had no intention of stopping there

They traded places more times than one could count
At times I couldn't breathe as they used me
      over and over

My tongue tired from extending

My body exhausted from the relentless use

My erections becoming sore and forced while
    my orgasms faded into being nearly dry and
    devoid of sensation

I didn't know if they were showing mercy
    commencing a sabbatical
    or they gave up when I nearly
    lost consciousness
I just remember waking from the fog of my own mind
    to the sounds of their kissing
    and
    their voices as bodies were enjoyed
    next to mine
I watched and felt an almost unwelcome pulse
    below my waist as
    my feeble body tried to ask for more
Wondering myself how much I could possibly take
    before my flesh would stop
    begging for it

Captain

There were moments she listened and
    obeyed
        but this was not one of them

She wasn't here to take orders

She was the captain of the ship

Prompt

A foot lifted and she rang the bell with a
      titchy toe
      before sitting back in her seat
Hearing the call from the next room over
      his clothes dropped to the
      hardwood floor
Laying in a pile he quickly walked away from
She had to force indifference onto the face
      that wanted so badly to smile from his
      prompt appearance
Not wanting to endure the consequences
      of his disobedience
He was trying his best
Knowing well and good that he was to be hard
      when entering the room

Cradled

Her groans left room for whimpers that
        slowly became quiet
I held still
Looking down as she moved forward to expose
        and pushed back to bury me in her
She leaned forward until her body released mine
I stood rigid
Shining with the reason for her song
She turned and opened her mouth to take
        all of me behind those red lips
Soft and
        incomprehensible whispers stimulated me
        with vibrations
Her tongue cradled the taste that was her pleasure
The flavor from inside of her faded into
        the taste of my skin
        and
        eventually she savored what she pulled
        from within me
I spilled over her tongue as that voice
        joyfully received the reward of the
        pleasure she gave

Wolves

There were wolves at the door
        but still
        she opened it
Letting them in because
        she was a lamb that wanted to be eaten
        and feel what it was like to be
        ripped to pieces by so many

Fathom

"Last night was amazing."
I said sitting down across from her
      at the local coffee shop
She looked at me
      in complete seriousness before speaking
"We're not finished."

I lifted my eyebrows before even taking a sip
"Oh?"

"You said that I could have everything, and I haven't
      had everything have I?
        Then we're not finished."

I locked my eyes onto hers
      swallowed heavily
      almost nervously
      and sat my mug down
That was when she finally started to crack a
      tiny
      deviant little smile
Confidently licking her lips and exhaling
      after a swallow of warmth
I just couldn't fathom what she
      could possibly be thinking

Windows

His fist in her hair
The beauty of her face pushed against the
      fog covered mirror
      as he fucked her
She reached a hand toward the glass to wipe it clean
      and
          nearly lost her balance as she did

It was building

It was boiling

The waves of sensation creeping towards the shore

It was a struggle
      but
      she kept her eyes open

Staring into the windows of her own soul
      as she started to cum all over his cock

Foreplay

That handshake
That smile
That was all the foreplay she needed

Flow

She stopped and lay on her side
      giving me that sexy look
      with her jaw dropped slightly
I walked on my knees to where that lovely face
      lay resting after working so hard on me

A smile

A nearly inaudible giggle

Her eyebrows lifting the smallest bit
      when she felt the heat land on her face
A curious tongue slowly reaching out
      from its hiding place as the warmth traveled
      down her cheek to flow between her lips

Skillet

She walked into the kitchen bare
His ever undeniable distraction
They tasted and took each other's
      newly woke bodies
        while the heat of an empty skillet
        cast its scent through the room

His intention was
      making breakfast for her to wake up to

Hers was to remind him why he did
      in the first place

Pushed

She was pushed down while
    he was pushing in
Both getting what they needed
    from each other
        at that very moment

Stunned

As late as it was we walked through the
      dark city streets
      hand in hand
Stopping to face her
      I was simply stunned by the
      sparkle in her eyes
The city lights reflecting from what she used
      to see me was a sight I wasn't ready for
The last time I saw that kind of twinkle in her eyes
      was that night
The very first night she invited me in and
      I made love to her

Turning

With lips together and
      mouths open
      they kissed on the busy sidewalk
Unaware of the activity bustling all around
Because to them
      there were only two souls that mattered
      and those
Those kept their tongues twirling
      as if the love they shared was the only reason
      the world was still turning

Timepiece

It wasn't like he could set his watch
        to when he was thinking about her
        because the thoughts never stopped
In fact
        there weren't enough numbers on the face
        of his timepiece
        to represent the amount of time he
        obsessed over her

Where I Dream

Through the haze of sleep she took
    silent steps in my direction
I struggled to see much more than those eyes
    but her bare skin insisted on
    radiating in a sense I couldn't quite understand
Lips met as fingers touched her face
    allowing the veil my mind kept her
    covered with
    to evaporate
I traced her silhouette with my eyes before
    feasting on the sight of the body before me
She wouldn't stand for our lips to be separated
    moving her mouth to mine
We loved repeatedly in any blessing
    her body allowed me to slide into
After which she looked at me and
    spoke without words
    "Where are we?"
I smiled and responded
    "This is where I dream, and I want you to stay
    here with me."

Sara

The sun rises in my heart
The clouds disappear and
> I swear the stars shine during the day
> when she looks at me
> and sends that smile my way

Through All

Slowly removing any clothing that covered
        the glow of
      early evening skin

I looked at her like she was the moon
        coming out from behind the clouds
      on a cold winter night

Promising that I as the sun would always
        seek to make her shine

Loving her heart through all of its phases

Foot Of Snow

It didn't need to be summer
These kinds of kisses could heat the air
    around them
      all on their own
Even with a foot of snow on the ground

Pulling

We danced with the moon
      just us in her light
She was so far but we held her so close
      we held her so tight
We allowed her to lead and
      our feet followed in strides
Her glow in my eyes and her gravity
      pulling at my lover's tides

Staircases

Her lips let me go when the
    shuddering and loss of control
    permeated my soul
At this point
    I could barely feel the kisses she continued
    to place

Addictively
    repeatedly tasting my
    exhausted softness

My head caught in a whirlwind

Spinning like
    cigarette smoke and
    spiral staircases

Obvious

Looking as innocent as innocence does
The mind in her head set fire to everything
      he thought would be at the will of his hand

Smiling confidently as his lips were licked
      after a sip from his drink

This was going to be fun

She smiled back like a mirror

It was obvious that he didn't know
      what he was in for

Invitation

He smiled
    kissed her
    and
    pushed
His face was warm and inviting
    but he was the one being invited in

Eternity

She was the most forbidden of sins
The unholy acts she allowed and even worse
      asked for and eventually
      begged me to do to every inch of the body
      God himself must have been so
      proud of creating

All were worthy of damnation and an
      eternity in Hell

So be it

Even I felt deserving of punishment after
      everything my hands
      all that my body and
      anything I could hold and reach her with
      had done to hers

New Life

Eyes that were comfortably haunting
    looked up at me

I hadn't ever seen this look

Those satiated irises

Those wet lips

She gazed at me like what
    she had just swallowed
        was giving her new life

Around the Corner

Nervousness flooded her veins as hands
    held onto bricks and eyes looked around
    the corner of the building
A couple were standing on the sidewalk having
    a conversation
She was sure they hadn't seen her
    but she was anxiety ridden
    nevertheless

The summer air caressed her backside as he
    held up her dress
She repeatedly peeked to assure herself that
    no one was walking in their direction
But she closed her eyes and hoped for the best
    when she felt something
    smooth and wet
    circle around and eventually
    push into her ass

He tasted the skin on the back of her neck
    while something firmer
    a finger
    and she was unsure which one
    stroked against her clitoris
She tried so hard not to make a sound
    when she came
    but staying completely silent
    was simply impossible

Ease

My hands wrapped around ankles
        as I held her legs back for our guest

I watched him penetrate her

I watched her stretch at his will

I watched a bottom lip tremble when
        her body uncontrollably quaked at the
        sum of his efforts

The sound of her weakened whimpering

The sound of their bodies as he used her

Who knows what was going through that mind
        behind the eyes she kept closed
Only opening them to look at mine as he
        emptied into her

The rise and fall of her chest as lungs desperately
        worked to keep her alive fed my soul

He left the room without a word as I let go
        and stepped around to where he was
Relief washed over her face as she reached up to
        touch mine

Tenderness in her eyes and a smile formed
    on her lips
    as my familiar flesh found it's way into hers

I slid in and out with an ease that was new to us both

She asked for me to
    and I couldn't stop from giving her mine as well

Wink

Laying in the sun she opened her mouth
    while looking at him and licking her lips

Winking

He stood
    excitedly dropping his trunks
She was only joking
    or was she
Giggling when he straddled the lawn chair and
    got closer with his semi-firm flesh
Wasting no time as he was behind her lips
    in the blink of an eye
Her toes spreading as he was now hard as a rock
    forcing her head into the backrest
    of the chair
Her nose filled with the scent of
    him and seawater

Thought

The motion of my wrist slowed
My lungs stuttered and altogether
    skipped a few breaths
I may have even whimpered
    the slightest bit
Whispering that name as I watched
    the thought of her roll down the
    back of my hand

Sticky

Following the scent in her nose
        and walking through the door
She loved watching him make breakfast
        nearly naked

He turned and handed over the cup of coffee he had
        brewed for her

She took that first sip as he continued cooking
Noticing the bulge in his boxer briefs
        as he turned
Thinking about how sticky his skin would be
        if she were to pour some syrup and
        lick it off of him down there

There was only one way to find out

Dark Hours

Her knees on the floor before the altar
      underneath a cross so similar to the one
      worn around her neck
A blessing of indiscernible words
      spoken by a man so holy
Lips parted and a tongue extended
      to receive the heavenly host
He felt the holy spirit move from
      base to tip and eventually
      flow from him
A burst at first and droplets afterwards that
      were wrung out of his flesh
      with the same hands she folded in prayer

She was blessed

She was saved
      and
She was happy to worship in any of the dark hours
      with him

Recents

She asked what I was doing after handing
    over her phone
I told her to sit back as it was tucked
    behind that waistband of her panties and
    pushed down
    slowly
    as far as it could go
Puzzled eyes changed to playful
    and eventually to
    slightly frustrated as it couldn't quite rest
    in the perfect spot
Her now frantic hands
    reached out to my pants
She could easily see that I was enjoying this
    as I used my phone to make sure that
    her "Recents" were filled with no name
    but mine

Open Curtains

Water droplets in their newfound freedom
    danced in the air above the
    liquid in my cup
She entered the room uncovered and bare
    as the frozen ground outside
    in this unusually snow-less winter
The plug she was wearing was visible as she
    casually leaned over the kitchen counter
Nearly offended by her apparently arrogant exhibition
    I stood and stepped into the air around her
    and
    calmed the chill of cool skin with fingertips that
    at first
    seemed to burn
Grabbing handfuls of flesh to hold her open
    and watch the jewel she wore
    shimmer in the light allowed in by
    open curtains
I like my tea strong
Giving it extra minutes to steep was only going to
    make my morning better

Wind

I asked for fingers to reach down
    and hold herself open
And as she did I gazed at her the way
    the sky would a butterfly
Allowing the breath I breathed while so close
    to be the wild
    warm
      flower filled wind

And my tongue

Held as broad
    flat and
    firm as I could make it
The long
    achingly slow taste I took
    from the bottom
    over her depth and
    up across where she could feel the most
That was the warm summer sunshine coming in
    through the window she opened for me

Patiently Waiting

She kept her mouth full
Refusing to swallow until the moment
    her forehead felt his kisses
    and
    her ears heard him say
    how good she made him feel

Numbers

I happened to catch a glimpse of her from
        across the coffee shop

Eye contact was held for a moment before
        it was broken by the greetings from
        a friend she must've been meeting there

I wasn't staring
        but I kept her smile in my peripheral

Thoughts racing through my mind of
        kissing her there
        there
        there
        and definitely everywhere under there

Those thoughts clouding everything so much that
        I barely noticed when she walked by
        and placed a napkin with some numbers
        at my table as they were leaving

Vernal

With a grin on my lips
        eyelids opened for irises to turn up toward her

Her body naked and glowing like a vernal sunrise

She stood above me with a shoe held to the
        center of my chest
        for feet such as these could never push
        bare souls to stand on something so dirty

The delicate rays of the sun in her gaze warmed
        every thread of my soul

Her smile forced the season of spring into me
        when she looked down and happily noticed
        that things were starting to grow

Stairwell

A few flights down where they thought
        it would be safe
They stripped each other down feverishly
        because neither could take the flirting
        any longer

Both wanting to fuck
        from the "Hello" they exchanged
        at the start of the evening

Enough was enough

Before anything was put into her she needed a taste
Her naked knees dropped
She had been sucking for what only
        seemed like seconds
        before he pulled her up by a fistful of hair
        and bent her over
She was as wet as he was hard as they collided
        in the stairwell

He felt the swelling build inside him as their ears
        heard voices below and the
        sound of shoes climbing stairs

She tightened around him in panic and he fucked
        as hard and
        as fast as he ever had

But still

He would rather be found than not finish in her

Soles

My knees touched the ground
    as she offered her bare feet
Her eyes closed and she remembered the way
    the ocean felt between her toes and the sand
    as I wrapped my mouth around them
    one at a time

Digging my tongue in to taste between each one

Eventually I stood before she smiled
    placing both feet on my stomach
    and moving them lower

She nearly giggled as they wrapped around
    my hard cock

Biting her lip when I held both tightly together
    and fucked them

The muscles in her legs tensing in an
    unimaginable grip as
    I sped up
    groaned
    and started to cum

Her gorgeous eyes never left mine
    as she used those feet
    to shine me with the semen on her soles

Watching me catch a breath as my blood flow
    tried returning to normal

Lens

Her hand wrapped around mine and I stood
    following her lead
I think we walked through two rooms before
    entering a third that contained a
    single chair

She had me sit
    before kneeling in front of me and
    giving her mouth to flesh that had already
    started to stand

As the impending rush began to cloud my senses
    she stopped
    stood and
    walked to the other side of a camera
    I didn't notice
    when we entered the room

She insisted that I finish myself while keeping my eyes
    fixated on the lens

Assuring me that she only wanted video of my face

I gave in to her request and started with a
    gentle grip on my shaft that slowly quickened

I stared at the light reflecting from the lens
    but could see the movement she tried to keep
    to herself in my peripheral

Her voice and the sounds she made
    were my reward
    when we seemed to exchange
    the deepest of breaths

Hers heard and
    mine seen by the mechanical eye
    documenting the moment for her
    future consumption

Down

Wrists bound
Eyes covered
Foam plugs expanding in her ears
    slowly taking away almost
    everything she could hear

A single finger led her lips to part as she
    knelt for so long it seemed like an eternity

He stepped toward a tongue that was
    dying to taste something
    anything
Filling that mouth and holding her head to keep it still
    while he worked

Every sound was deafening behind the plugs
    in her ears

Her heart beating like a hammer in her head

One that she thought was going to burst
    through her chest
    when an unfamiliar pair of hands landed
    on her back and
    slowly started moving down

Depravity

He treated her fantasies with care
      as he wished for her to do with his
Intimacy of this level was rarely available
      to tether souls together
But the vile things they dug in to speak of
      were exchanged without shame
Because even depravity deserves to be
      handled delicately

Flower

She held the covers open and read out loud
      topless
Turning pages one after another
Visualizing the love they were making
      in those words

Her bare chest soaking up the sunlight like a flower
      begging for food

She daydreamed about being there with them
Floating
Fucking
      and
      being fucked as in the dreams she had
      while her eyelids were closed

Treat

He crawled
      without a thread of clothing covering his skin
      to where she sat
Lips kissed from where her feet
      touched the floor
      up to her parted knees
When his head was just past them
      she reached down to stop him
Lifting his head to see that desperate expression
How adorable were those puppy-dog eyes
      when they looked at hers before softly asking
      "Please?"
Why not?
He was being such a good boy
She thought he deserved a treat

Experience

Insisting I lay back
    the both of them met at my midsection
Their eye contact couldn't be broken
I had been inside both of them and they
    insisted on finishing me together
It was beautiful to watch a married couple
    work together towards a common goal
He tried to play it off
His apprehension was clearly on display
    but
    she supported him throughout
Taking turns with mouths
    their eyes watched one another do their best
    until the teamwork paid off
They both took part in cleaning me
    and
    shared special kisses as I grew limp
I left with a hug from one and
    a handshake from the other
Both thanking me for allowing the experience
    they had just shared
Holding hands while walking me to the door

Frantic

Shoes splattered on rain-soaked sidewalks
The soft October air cradled the smiles
    they gave one another

All until one smile was too much

She pushed him against the wall of
    some unknown building
Slightly knocking the back of his head
    but sealing his lips with hers before he could
    exclaim from the pain

Hands quickly became frantic

Overcoats explored before he pulled her
    around the corner
The lips on her face grinning with the knowledge
    of his intention
As soon as they could find a spot that was
    out of sight

Shot

He provided her morning shot
    and it wasn't espresso
It gave so much more energy

Knowing

Entering the room to the aroma
    of freshly brewed coffee
She sipped from her favorite mug
    while I peered through the steam
    to drink from her eyes
Porcelain hid her lips from my sight
    but I smiled all the same
Knowing exactly what she could do with that mouth

Boastful

Oh
The things these boastful bedroom mirrors
    would love to say they've seen

As I

Knees on the floor
Wrists bound behind her
Mouth open
Tongue caressing my skin
Hair pulled as I
      force fed her throat

Door

Her hands held the door open
      and he responded politely
A warm smile greeted her
      as he came inside
She couldn't wait to show him even more hospitality

That Stare

Every last drop was gone and the way he stood
        in front of her spoke of how
      weak she had made him

Finally he dropped to unsteady knees
Head in her lap
Her fingers running through his hair like he was
        some kind of pet

She looked at me with so much pride
        it bordered on arrogance

That stare caused a chill to run down my spine

I stood in defiance
        taking a step towards her

Telling myself I could handle it so much better than he

But when fingers wrapped around me
        and that first kiss touched my skin
        I wasn't so sure anymore

Catching Rain

That voice of hers was thunder
      but the sinful things she spoke of
      were lightning strikes
She held out her hand
      looked in my eyes and so politely asked
      the wind in my heavy breaths
      to give her the chance to catch rain
      in the palm of her hand

Prints

It still burned when tired hands pulled those
        pretty
        polka dot panties
        up to cover purple and pink paddle prints

Her mind was filled with him throughout the day as
        sensitive skin was swaddled by her clothing

A soreness was felt whenever she sat
        but her mind tingled and
        a smile curled the corners of her lips
        as the memories the pain
        started to make her wet

Marks

She wanted the lights low
      so that I wouldn't see
      the marks that life had given
      to her skin over children and years
But even in the darkness I would feel for them
      like they were put there for my hands to grip
      while I loved her hard enough
      for her mind to forget that they
      were even there

Wings

That celestial voice echoed between these walls
        as we loved

My thumb drawing halos around her
        while the body I was slowly sliding in and out of
        shook and trembled at my touch

The flow I could no longer suppress
        matched the warmth she held around me
I watched lips quiver and a fair-skinned chest
        rise and fall heavily
Knowing at that moment something new
        had been created

She had been given wings

She was taking her very first breaths after
        becoming an angel

Down Below

They had only begun
    but the rope that was
    placed and laced through
    had already started to affect her

Every wrap and tie became a cloud
    in her mind

And at times she swore there were gusts of wind
    under her new wings
When blindfolded and immobile her heart
    knew she was flying and
    there was nothing on the earth that could
    convince her otherwise
Gliding and drifting across the sky while
    her problems and concerns
    failed to grasp at her
    from so far down below

Oceana

The salty taste of sweaty skin made her
    think of the sea

Even when a thousand miles from the shore

Savoring the waves that crashed onto her tongue
    when he growled like distant thunder
    was the essence of oceana

Being A Brat

There had been several times
    I warned her not to wear it

That was my favorite hoodie

Still she seemed to enjoy taunting me
    with the way it draped over her frame
She walked out of the room towards the kitchen
    and I followed quietly
    a few steps behind
Startling her with a hand on the center of her back
    pushing her toward the counter

The leggings she wore desperately tried to hang
    onto her legs

Failing
    of course as I nearly pulled them to the floor

I used only my saliva to push a finger into her
    before shining myself and pushing until I was
    completely buried

That first gasp quickly changed
    to a growl
    and then that intentional
    giggle

I warned her

I told her exactly what I would do
．．．．．but she seemed to think it was funny

She was being a brat so I grabbed
．．．．．a hip with one hand
．．．．．her hair with the other and
．．．．．proceeded to fuck her ass
．．．．．right there against the kitchen island

Silence

There was an excitement that arrived
      when his tongue remained still

She took a deep breath and closed her eyes

Her body itched with anticipation
      tingled in preparation
The skin that covered her knew that when his lips
      spoke in nothing but silence
      he was planning

He would be saying everything with his hands

Captured

Looking over her shoulder those eyes
       stalked
       hunted and
       captured mine

Holding me hostage

With every essence of the word she was
       fucking me with those eyes
I couldn't look away and
       I couldn't keeping my body from reacting
There was a tightness between my legs
I shoved hands into my pockets to obscure
       what was happening to me
This was getting serious

Early Grave

Lingerie adorned her pale skin with black lace
        and a contrast that was
          striking to the eyes
Her makeup flawless as I couldn't distract myself
        from those dark red lips
I removed one article of clothing at a time
        while she watched with a grin

A sparkle in her eyes that she
        just couldn't suppress
        regardless of how hard she tried to

An outstretched hand summoned me and
        she took my flesh in her fingers
She didn't speak
        but her eyes were demanding that I did

"It's yours. Do whatever you like."

Her crimson lips parted slightly as she sent
        the smile that tried to show me
        to an early grave

Shadows

Caught on the outside
      wearing only shadows
I took her hand
Undressing this body by leading her
      into the light
To a place where shadows couldn't be
A place where delightful darkness radiated
      as brightly as the sun

Buckles

Buckles were fastened and she swung her hips
      the smallest bit before looking down
      and wrapping her hands around it
Droplets from the bottle reflected the warm glow
      provided by pillars and tea lights as she
      shined what she was wearing
Excited fingertips gave him a shine as well
      before she held it there
      and began to push
Biting her own lip as she watched what hung
      from the harness between her legs
      slowly dis and reappear
She leaned forward and nibbled his ear with
      her chest to his back
      as he tried to suppress a soft groan
      that became a growl
Repeatedly pushing in and out before reaching
      around his waist
      between
      his skin and the sheets
      with a hand that was still slick

Just to check and see

Smiling at what she found

First Time

Kneeling in front of the mirror
      eyes found themselves as
      fingers discovered another part of her
She took her time as the
      house was quiet
Fingertips unfolded her flesh like a
      prized piece of chocolate

Finding sweetness and thoroughly tasting it by touch

The swelling
The rush came closer
      and as the sensation overtook her body
      she stayed focused on the eyes
Long enough to see that they had softened
And when she found the nerve to look at her
      entire face
      she grinned at what she saw

She was smiling and glowing

Others had seen her in this state
      but this was her first time

Knelt

Sitting comfortably
Legs crossed
A fluid movement flung the heel worn
    by her left foot to the other side of the room
I stooped and eventually
    knelt
Kissing her toes ever so lightly
    tasting between them
Lifting my eyebrows and
    letting my gaze find hers
    as I took the largest into my mouth
Looking up at her eyes the same way
    hers pierce mine when she takes me
    behind those lips

Give It

They embraced and her arms wrapped around
    his neck
A kiss broken as her jaw dropped
    with an involuntary gasp
He had reached around and clenched a grip
    on her backside
    like it was already his
And all she wanted to do was
    put her face down
    hold it open
    and give it to him

Into Flames

The stubble of the face he had shaven
      one day before
      scratched at her skin as he slowly kissed
      from her knee to her inner thigh
Like a match being scraped along the
      side of the box
      so slowly it couldn't ignite

All while she was ready

So ready
      to burst into flames

Swirled

Just as he was asked
      his clothes were removed before sitting

She sat next to that naked lap and kissed his lips

Softly at first
      reaching down to hold him
Despite the slow speed at which she moved
      he still grew to fill her hand
The kisses stopped for a moment
      while she smiled and
      watched his eyes roll back before closing

The reaction that was always received
      when her thumb swirled and
      spread the tears of his hunger
      as she gently tugged and twisted
      with her other hand

Angels

The line moved slowly

Each leaving their wings at the door as they
        stepped through to find her
        with a grin on her face and
        ankles raised and separated before
        she invited them in

Each stayed only a few moments

But every one of them
        left the taste of near-divinity on her tongue
        and a gift from heaven within her
One she could feel trickling out slowly
        to collect as a puddle
        of the kingdom of God beneath her

More so with every angel she allowed to
        enter the room

Prey

You wear this silk around your eyes so beautifully
Now that I've brought you into darkness
      open them

See the world you want

Take a breath
      clear your mind and
      open your heart
Leave your shame and inhibitions
      for they are not welcome here

Show me everything you hide

I want to see the animal I know you are

That's it

Good girl

Now my darling
Come claim your prey

Pitiful

She brought her mouth close but
      her lips never touched him
Fingernails traced and swirled around him softly
      as the flesh they teased
      tensed and twitched

He begged for a grip to wrap around his starving skin

She spoke not to him
      but to the body at her fingertips
      of all the disgusting things she could do
Her tongue so close but all he could feel was
      the breath of her words and the
      sharp sensation of her nails
After letting him suffer for so long her hand
      wrapped around him and
      the tiniest movements she made were relief
      from the tension

Fluid came leaping from him

Some even catching and hanging on her
      bottom lip
To this she let go
      stepped back and let him know
      how pitiful he looked
      straining and leaking all over himself

Pace

She knew it was close so she kept
    grinding on him

Quickening the pace

Biting his lip and stretching it from his mouth
    as he shook
    twitched and
    trembled within her

Unlocking

That tongue knew me
      inside and out
My grooves
My edges
The way I tasted when it was
      impossible to hold back any longer

it was the key she kept with her
      at all times

Using any moment she could to
      leave my face flushed and
      my heart hammering

She insisted on pulling me away and unlocking me

Regardless of who we might run into
      or the chance that she might get caught

My Perfect Mess

Taking a step back
      I admire the angel on my sheets
      as she struggles to smile back at me

The pale complexion that covered her was
      mottled from my grip
      like a pink hydrangea

Her afterglow sparkling as sunlight reflected from the
      sweat
      saliva and
      semen on her skin

My perfect mess

Full

Her eyes looked down at his with an almost
    mischievous anticipation
        as she repeatedly slid up and down his shaft
They each grinned in agreement before
    she sat up
    turned and
    sent a nod to invite their guest

"Slowly"

Spoken with a smile before placing her hands
    back onto the sheets at his shoulders

The mattress shook slightly as he moved in
    behind her
She tried to breathe calmly as his head breached
    the flesh in which her lover already resided
    but her lungs stayed full
Each inch was felt with an almost new set of senses
    as he joined them

When stretched completely she let go of the
    longest exhale she could ever remember
    before they started to fuck her
    one after another

The sensation of them struggling
      fighting to stay inside her body
      set her mind on fire

Just the thought of their hard cocks pushing against
      one another with nothing but the
      liquor of her lust
      between them was a trigger like none she had
      ever known

Her body burst with an intensity she hadn't felt
      before or since
Falling limp onto his chest and simply breathing while
      they continued fucking her
      stretching her
      pushing into her until one finished
It was impossible to tell which
      but the second followed shortly

Their combined gasps sounded like a storm

She felt so full even as they twitched and softened

When all was over they rolled her over onto the bed
One covering her with blankets while their guest
      placed a pillow underneath her weary head

She looked at them one at a time with a
      satiated smile
      while an absolute flood flowed from her flesh
      where neither of them could see

Leaves

My hands wrapped around her throat and
        I fucked until there was nothing left of her
        and she lay growling on the floor
Shaking like the shadows of wind blown leaves
        holding onto me like a branch
          they were trying so hard not to let go of

Discovery

The scent of her hair was always welcome
    to any breath he brought in
Especially when her hand reached behind
    to feel him getting hard

Simply

The look in your eyes is fire
      and even the memory of your mouth
      on my skin
      melts me
And when you moan while keeping contact
      when those lips make me yours
      I simply burn

Ours

She held me in place and I pushed slowly
Taking every necessary second for each
      gentle movement
I kept my eyes open to watch her face relax
      and her body sink deeper into the bedding
A beautiful sight drenched in the buttery sunlight
      of a cold December afternoon
      that was meandering towards early evening
We melted into and
      became one another
The heavy rush of it all causing motions to
      feel like warm liquid
      as we released ours

Music

Her perfume
      red nails and
      tasteful tattoos
Inviting his hands to the piano
      to play and force beautiful music from her
Lured in by the rose petals strewn across the keys

Dolls

Canvas on the easel
Colors on the bristles of brushes
She painted a world where her lovers
    didn't choose to leave
One where she could keep and
    collect them all

Having them play like dolls that were naked together

Watching their hands wander until all were hard
    and they used each other's bodies
    in front of her

Eventually her clothes would drop to the floor
    and her bare feet would carry her
    into the center of their gathering
That was when she became the focus of
    all those hands
    all those lips
    among other things

Driven

Her sweet voice held in silence with a ball
Wrists and ankles joined together by rope
      that helped keep her still
He slowly paced around his willing and
      most prized possession
      holding eye contact when he could
He disappeared from her sight but his presence
      was always known

His touch somehow burned with gentleness

The air from his lungs brushed against
      places she so badly wanted to be tasted
Her skin was on fire with goose flesh to the point
      that it was seemingly reaching out to bring
      his hands to touch her

But this man possessed an amount of patience
      she didn't think was possible

He was driven by it
      and that in itself was simply terrifying

Fingertips

Her heart waited its whole life to be heard
He listened the way she needed him to
With open ears
      tender eyes
      a firm grip and
      well versed fingertips

Embraced

In those arms she embraced the role of being
    his kitten
    his good girl
    his little one
And while he held her
It was known that his duty was to keep her
    calm
    safe and
    wet

In Reality

He led her into so many dark
        pitch black places
The thoughts in her mind
The wishing in her soul
Places that were so dark
        yet
        he somehow filled with
        nothing but the most wonderful light

Smaller

She had an idea of
      how many licks
      it would take before her tongue tasted
      what he held hidden inside
But still
Every time she had him there
      the goal was a smaller number

Tool

A circle of pins traveled across the surface
    of her skin
The wayfaring wheel traversed the topography of her

Leaving behind
    a trail of tiny indentations
    wherever it went

So many paths were mild and
    barely felt

While others blazed with nerve shattering fire

All left this body begging for a deeper penetration
    than this tiny tool could ever offer

Never Were

Never were
      the sting of his hands
      the impact of leather falls or
      the burden of chains as heavy on her body
      as the weight his eyes held on her heart

Invited

Her ass raised effortlessly
    from where she was laying
Allowing him the space to easily remove those
    black
    lace
    panties
She might as well have just
    unlocked
    opened the door and
    invited in a vampire

Kisses

Sometimes she wanted kisses that were sweet
    and soft

But other times she needed kisses that were "more"

And "more" started when
    her jaw dropped
    her eyes lit up and
    his hands wrapped around her throat

Call In

My hand traveling between sheets and skin
      as the early light of a rainy morning
          fought to find its way through closed curtains

I find a beautiful ass and uncover her
      to bestow kisses that began softly
      and
      grew slowly into bite marks as a free hand
      rubbed between her legs
Fingers finding her easily as she had held onto
      the lust I placed into her before sleeping

So slick
      warm and
      smooth around my touch

Her voice trying to speak with vocal chords that
        weren't yet awake
Firm circles and zigzags were slowly pushed across
      her epicenter with ease
The morning storm failing to compete with the
      puddles and thunder I dragged from her
      sleepy body

Giving kisses to the smile on her lips before leaving
      to start my shift
Her hands holding onto me tightly as that tired voice
      asked me to call in for the day

Hunger

That first pass
      of my hand over your ass
      sets my soul on fire
Hunger pains
      from what happens in my brain
      sets the path of my desire

Never

"God damn that smell never gets old."
She thought to herself as he approached
      with only a towel
         around his waist
She pressed her face against his tacky skin
      and for who knows how long
         just breathed in and out
Breaking the silence as her teeth sank into him
      without a second thought

Rope

A rope wasn't needed
The mind inside his head already knew
    that he had a hold on her heart
He just didn't want reflexes and reactions
    persuading her into wiggling away
    as she had a tendency of trying to do
She was going to stay right there and take everything
    he was planning to give her
It was time to feel the
    intensity of his intentions

That's what the rope was for

Smoldering

The energy of his presence
The strength of his hands
The power in the placement of every fingerprint
      that was left smoldering on this scorched skin
She felt so small while her body was
      consumed by the command in his touch

Public

Often times I caught myself
    in busy
    public places
Stepping close enough to place a hand
    on her backside and
        lean forward to inhale the scent of her hair

Somewhere Else

Lips
      teeth and
      tongue
      met the skin between her shoulder and scalp
His mouth fed from her neck
      but she swore to God that her body was
      feeling kisses somewhere else

Heroine

She dropped to naked knees
    exhaling audibly
He looked down to catch teeth biting a red lower lip
    as confident hands tugged at the elastic
    of what kept him covered

From the very first touch he knew

She was no damsel in distress
    that needed saving

She was the motherfucking heroine

Breath

The weather was calm
      but that single breath
The exhale that escaped him when he
      looked down
      lifted and
      held her ankles so far apart
      could have been a hurricane

Oleander

She bloomed after the sun set on an
      August afternoon
Ornate in my garden and
      glowing by the light of the moon

I struggled
      by touch
      by sight
      by scent
      and failed to identify her

Not a lily or rose
      nor lavender

Much more like oleander

Tethered

A clamp on the right
      followed by one on the left
What tethered the two together was tucked
      between her teeth giving them
      a gentle
      yet
      assertive pull

Wrists were tied above her head before
      the lashings began

His voice unusually authoritative
      but it turned her on so
Telling her that things would get rougher if she
      couldn't keep that chain between her teeth

With him speaking so sternly in that tone
      there was no choice but to believe him

Someone Else

From the way her lips welcomed me
        to the way her fingers wrapped
        around my flesh

Everything felt different

It was like she was someone else
        with that blindfold on
I didn't need to
        but thought it would be fun to know
        who she was thinking about
        under there

Lulls

Let me gaze upon you with the sun
      at my back
Your fingers gently unfolding
      the petals of a flower
Watching the changes as you
      grow through spring
      bloom in the heat of summer
      and
      settle to rest as autumn's air lulls you to sleep

Pure Control

Pulling his voice
      his groans and
      her name
      from his throat and past his lips was so easy

It brought her so much joy

Her hand
      mouth and
      the combination of the two
      assured any moment
      would be filled with hymns from him

His moans changed to whimpers before
      begging to fuck her

That was up to her and
      whether or not she decided to take it from him
      right now
      or let him push it into her
      forced that familiar feeling between her legs
For now she sang along with her own voice
      against his most sensitive skin
      until she made up her mind

Letting

My spent flesh rested against her as I
        crawled up her back
There was very little acknowledgment
        of my presence
        as the skin of her soft shoulder was kissed

She slipped into unconsciousness as the
        remnants of spasms slid from her
        and onto the sheets

I stood and stared for who knows how long
        before covering her with the comforter
        and letting her dream

Undoubtedly

After all these years ropes and chains
      weren't necessary for him to claim
      the submission of her

She was so undoubtedly his

But still he loved catching and tying her
And in a similar way she adored being captured
      and watching him tie the ropes to keep her still

Even more did she enjoy
      watching him
      listening to him
      feeling him exhaust his body in hers
      wherever he chose to

That was when she was truly his
      and she knew she had a hand around his heart

Even when she couldn't move to touch him

Champagne

Opening bottles of champagne
    was always appropriate
There was never a night that their love
    wouldn't be worthy of celebration

Song

She knew every lyric
She knew every note by heart
Lips wrapped around and
      her tongue pressed against
        skin she owned but wasn't at all hers
He heard the familiar melody and
      in his mind
        he sang along
Heart pounding
      flesh growing long
        while he felt everything and
        she hummed her favorite song

Hidden

This was it
That tongue and those fingers were exactly
    where she wanted them to be
In and exhales that were breaths she kept
    tucked away

Hidden in secret places just for moments like these

Universes

Palms seemed to glow with the
        flame and
        heat of the
        fire that engulfed my soul when she
        used them on me

The light of the creator she is radiated
        from those hands
        as she made me see stars
        and forced my senses to feel them flow

Her waiting tongue collecting the
        universes she demanded from me
        to again become one with she who made them

Ride

She braced her arms and
      held her legs stiff to
      slightly push back
Knowing that when she felt him grab hair
      with one hand and
      flesh with another
He was going to take her for a ride

Surprise

Steam slowly escaped as she silently stared through
        the separation of the shower curtain
Watching water fall down his back and
        rinse away the lather that made his skin
        smell so damn good
She closed the curtain and quietly undressed
        before stepping in to surprise warm flesh with
        cold hands
Pushing him against the wall before dropping
        to her knees behind him
Ready to use her tongue in a way
        she never had before

In Places

Her eyes were fixated on his hands
      as he sipped from the old fashioned
      in his glass

Just making sure they were still there

She knew it was impossible

But when his eyes looked into hers
      it felt like he was touching her body
      in places he couldn't possibly reach
      from where he was sitting

Lampshade

Simple white undergarments matched so well
    with the cozy sweater she left on

Bare legs lifted as hands
    clutched
    pushed and
    turned circles between them

I stood silent and still

Fighting to hear her breaths through my own

A gentle voice purring softly as I watched
    those panties darken slightly
    under her fingertips

The fabric absorbed everything her
    body couldn't contain

The sweetness of thoughts in her head
    and the pressure of her own touch
    collecting in the cotton and shining
    like warm light through a lampshade

To Memory

She looked at his enamoration standing
    inches from her face
She smelled him
She tasted him
She watched the way his skin traversed firm flesh
    when
        her hand wrapped around and
        moved up and down
And when pearls appeared before rolling
    from him and over her skin
She closed her eyes and
    committed it all to memory

Blooming

Eyes watering slightly

My left hand pinning her to the bed
       by the throat
My right between trembling legs that could barely
       at this point
       hold themselves apart
Soaked and saturated so much so that
       the nerves in my fingers could feel little more
       than the faintest details such slick skin
       would allow

Maybe this would be the last one
       maybe it wouldn't

But she cried out and I grew hard with
       the sound of her lungs trying to give her breath
       the quickened pulse in my grip and
       the sight of her cheeks and chest changing
       from pale to red

Like a field of roses blooming all at once

His

When ropes held her tight
    she didn't have to think
She didn't have to move
She didn't have to worry
She didn't have to be anything for the world
When she was tied
    she could only be one thing

His

Please

I promised only to watch

She was laying fetal on the mattress when
       her hand came behind
       lifting and showing me those gorgeous
       pastel pink petals
       just to tease me

I watched one finger disappear
       then another

She massaged the shimmer of oil over and into her
Highlighting visible skin with the light that
       shined in from the window behind me

Those frail fingers kept vanishing into her
       until none could be seen
Only her wrist was visible as she rocked against
       the end of her arm

I was throbbing and dying for release

I asked first
       to which she replied "Please."

I stood and finished myself on the hand
       that could be seen one moment
       and not the next

Portions of my fluid being consumed by
    the movements she made

The rest pushed back as she
    shook
    held so still and
    eventually withdrew

Smiling as I stooped to taste her fingers

Explore

Hours passed and the initial
    awkwardness
    conversation and
    drinks in public came to an end
Leading to her sofa and a film they couldn't stop
    talking through
Credits rolled as he stood to
    bow out and respectfully
    conclude the evening
To his surprise
    she rose to her socked feet
Taking a step to close the distance between them

Her lips close enough to kiss
    but they merely exchanged breaths as
    the sounds of her fingers releasing the button
    of the tight jeans she wore rang in his ears
She removed them
    sat back down and
    glanced at his slowly flushing face in approval

Her knees parted as he fell to his

She could tell by the breaths his lungs took
    that he could smell her desire
    before he seemed to whisper with
    those first touches

Looking down
    her eyes watched him
      explore and discover her
One fingerprint at a time

Thank you.

Appreciation is always appropriate and right now I am overflowing with it. The wonderful cover of this book was made by the multi-talented Alex at ABC Design. I would also like to thank all of the family and friends that continue to lift me up with support and encouragement.

I would also like to express my gratitude to all of the page owners, social media supporters, and fellow authors and creators for sharing my work in your corner of the world, wherever you may be.

I would love to thank everyone individually, by name, but at the risk of missing someone, I'm not even going to attempt it.

However, there is one person that I will acknowledge by name. My beautiful Sara. This is for you. Every morning I wake up and you're right there for me to give my heart to. Your faith in me and my work is absolutely priceless. Thank you for not killing me for hiding all those plastic bugs . . . :)